TO TIDDLES

First published 2010 by Walker Books Ltd
87 Vauxhall Walk, London SE11 5HJ

2 4 6 8 10 9 7 5 3 1

© 2010 Charlotte Voake

The right of Charlotte Voake to be identified as author/illustrator
of this work has been asserted by her in accordance with the
Copyright, Designs and Patents Act 1988

This book has been typeset in Calligraphic 810

Printed in China

British Library Cataloguing in Publication Data:
a catalogue record for this book
is available from the British Library

ISBN 978-1-4063-2238-5

www.walker.co.uk

GINGER
and the mystery visitor

WALKER BOOKS
AND SUBSIDIARIES
LONDON · BOSTON · SYDNEY · AUCKLAND

Charlotte Voake

Ginger and the kitten
were very lucky cats.

They lived with
a little girl
who took great
care of them.

Here she is,
giving them
breakfast ...

a big bowl
for Ginger

and a little saucer
for the kitten.

But Ginger and the kitten
aren't the only ones
who like the look
of a nice
breakfast.

Someone
is watching them
through the
window!

"I wonder who that is?" said the little girl, but nobody knew.

The visitor just stared
through the window,
watching Ginger
and the kitten
eat their
delicious meals.

Then one day,
they found him
in the kitchen,
licking out
their bowls.

When he had finished,
he gave himself
a wash ...

and left!

Whenever the door
was open,
in he came.

Once, Ginger
found him asleep
on the bed!

But the visitor never stayed long and he never forgot to check the dishes, on his way in or out.

"I wonder where
he comes from?"
said the little girl.
"I wonder where he goes?
I hope he's got someone nice
to look after him."

And then she had an idea.

She found
a piece of paper
and a bit
of ribbon,
and on the
paper
she wrote:

Do I belong to anyone?

The next time
he visited,
she folded the
paper and tied
it round
his neck.

"Now we have
to wait,"
she said.

Ginger and the kitten had just finished eating supper when their visitor came to the window.

He looked
very
hungry.

He still
had the ribbon
round his neck.

But on the ribbon was a *different* piece of paper.

It was a reply, and this is what it said:

My name is Tiddles. I have a loving home and two square meals a day. Please do not feed me as I am getting rather fat.

"TIDDLES?" said the little girl. "Tiddles, what a cheeky little cat you are!"

Tiddles looked up at her.

"No, Tiddles," she said. "No more food for you!"

Tiddles just stared
hopefully
at the
empty dishes.

Poor Tiddles!
The little girl would not
let him in,
however sadly
he stared through the window.

"I'm sorry, Tiddles,
you have
a home of your own,"
she said.

Tiddles came to the window less and less.

Then he stopped visiting altogether.

But Ginger and the kitten
saw him quite often,
sometimes next door,
sometimes at the school
down the road ...

up to his tricks
again.

"Here's our old friend!"
everyone said,
and Tiddles
was very happy.

But wherever Tiddles visited,
he never stayed too long ...

because, of course,
he had his own dinner
waiting for him ...

at HOME!